"The Christmas Pirate"^{TM}
Story, Images, and Artwork © 2001 by Gregory J

Cover Illustration by - Jon DeGorsky
Edited by - Jon DeGorsky

All rights reserved.

For additional information, and products visit **www.thechristmaspirate.com**

Published by: **Magnetic Image, Inc.**
www.magneticimagestudios.com

Printed in the United States of America

Library of Congress Cataloging-in-Publication Data

"The Christmas Pirate"^{TM} first printing 2007
Revised Edition 2008

ISBN 0-9678542-3-7

10 9 8 7 6 5 4 3 2 1

2

Isle of Rumors

It began long, long ago on a far away island by the name of Isle Par-tend. On this island, a young boy dreamed of sailing the ocean blue.

"Oh how I wish my father would let me sail with him. I know I am strong enough to help him and his crew", said the young Chris Masterson, son of Captain Masterson. Chris was always looking out his bedroom window, staring over the endless ocean, imagining he was a great captain like his father. He began to wring his hands like a greedy pirate and said aloud, "Someday I will get my chance to sail my own ship. I will call her 'Blue Sea', the ship of many gifts. When I sail upon the ocean everyone will look forward to my arrival."

8

One late, stormy night, a knock came to the door. As Chris's mother opened the door, he could see two large figures. Suddenly, his mother let out a cry and fell to her knees. Captain Masterson was lost at sea.

10

As the years slipped by with no word of Chris's father, many rumors spread across the island. One such rumor claimed that Captain Masterson's ship sank to the bottom of the ocean during a nasty storm. Another rumor claimed his ship was taken over by ruthless pirates.

12

As these terrible rumors continued to spread, Chris continued to stare hopefully out his bedroom window every night. He could only think of his father's safe return. "I know what happened," Chris thought to himself one night, "Pirates took over his ship because there were so many gifts aboard."

14

One early morning, as the sun began to rise up on the shore, a loud clanking sound could be heard across the whole island, or so it seemed. It was Chris Masterson, now a young man around eighteen years old. He was working as a dockhand, planning to castaway aboard a ship. Once he was on board, he planned to find his way to the far off island where he was certain pirates were holding his father captive.

When no one was looking, Chris snuck aboard the mighty ship, The Surveyor, which was captained by none other than the great Captain Tourik. Captain Tourik was known for his fierce temper, and if Chris was caught aboard as a stowaway, he would certainly be thrown overboard to the sharks.

18

On The Surveyor's last day at sea, just as the ship was pulling into port, something happened that would change Chris's life forever. Captain Tourik walked over and opened the bulk head to where Chris was hiding, slowly leaned forward, and said with a loud, gruff voice, "Come here boy." It seemed that Captain Tourik was aware of Chris being onboard the whole time, as well as why he was there in the first place.

20

"Arr, boy!" the Captain shouted, "You need not tell me a thing, but listen here. I will help you, and in return you must do one thing for me. You must bring my son a gift that I had promised long ago." Without hesitation, perhaps out of fear, Chris said yes.

Chris stayed onboard The Surveyor for nearly two years learning the ways of the sea under the great captain. He became a very capable sailor and even learned to captain his own ship. Once the time came for Chris to go his own way, Captain Tourik gave Chris a sack that contained the gift for his son, for he did not forget the deal they made two years ago in that open bulk head.

24

Chris left the ship in search of his very own and quickly found one on Bluff Island, where he and the captain parted ways. Sitting outside a ship was an old captain boasting about how great a chance taker he was. Chris needed this ship, so he said to the old captain, "For your ship, I bet I can run up the stern line, jump to the helm, and come back again without breaking two fresh eggs."

The old captain looked to him and said, "My eyes have never seen such a thing, boy. You've got yerself a deal, but under one condition. If either egg cracks even a bit, you'll be my new ship hand for two years without pay." The old captain didn't realize that Chris had wrapped the eggs and placed them under his hat.

As Chris ran back and forth across the ship, not an egg cracked. The captain yelled out, "You're a red flag and a half moon, boy! Dangerous, aye, but only half true. What be your name?" "My name is Chris Masterson," Chris eagerly replied. "All right then Captain Masss… Massser… oh heck, I'll likely only remember a red flag and a half moon," said the old captain as they shook hands.

Captain Chris, now aboard his new ship named Gloria, after his dearest mother, searched many strange places and saw many strange things. At every port his father wasn't, Chris collected special trinkets to remember where he had been. During his travels, though, he never forgot his promise to Captain Tourik.

32

One day, the skies were filled with dark green clouds, signaling a very bad storm ahead. Captain Chris continued on, however, for he was on course to an island that he had heard housed a crazy old man. A crazy old man that Chris thought to be his father.

34

Captain Chris's ship had survived the storm, and had arrived at the island. An eerie silence was abound. No gulls singing, no sounds coming from the island, not even the sound of the sea could be heard. From the dock, a sign reading "Beware, Isle of Rumors" was barely visible. One of the crewmen of the ship yelled out, "There seems to be some crewmen missing! They must have been blown overboard in the storm, captain!"

At the thought of finally finding his father, Captain Chris paid no attention to the calls and went ashore with a few men.

38

Chris and his men headed to a local pub, not far from the eerie docks. Inside, several locals were giving the men strange looks and acting odd. Ignoring this, the men swaggered up to a table and yelled, "Give here a drink, and a round for all!" At once the strange looks turned to cheers, for they were happy to drink for free.

40

As time passed the locals began to brew a story about Captain Chris and the crewmen lost during the storm. A man came up to Captain Chris in the pub while the captain was talking to a crewman about the lowering morale among his fellow crewmen. The man sat next to Captain Chris and said, "I hear ye are as crazy as the old man up on the hill."

42

Excited to hear about the man he had been looking for, Captain Chris played along and said, "Yes, yes I am. Please tell me about this old man." The man laughed and said, "Well he's crazy I tell ya. Went crazy near when he come here. No one will go near him for fear they'll catch it. Lives up on that hill. Only but one house, can't miss it."

44

Captain Chris left the pub and started up the hill to the crazy man's house. He quickly found himself in front of a window where he saw a shadow within. Captain Chris barged through the door yelling, "Who are you?" At that very moment, he felt a large thump to his head, and darkness fell upon his eyes.

46

Moments later, Captain Chris opened his eyes only to find a beautiful young lady standing above him. "How dare you barge into my home like that and scare me!" exclaimed the young lady. Captain Chris looked at her and said, "I'm very sorry malady... and so is my head."

48

The young lady walked toward the window, shifted her gaze toward the trees, and said to Captain Chris, "The old man that lives here hit you. He thought you were an intruder trying to get to me. He really is a very nice man. He's like a father to me. Always has been, ever since he saved me from the mob.

50

A few years back, the island people were forcing me to marry a man I did not know or love. When I resisted they came to get me, but I fled. I knew I would be safe with the old man since all the townspeople thought he was crazy. I wouldn't be bothered here, and in return for keeping me safe from the angry mob, I take care of him."

Captain Chris gazed at the young lady and asked, "What is your name?" "Yolanda," she replied. At that very moment Captain Chris fell in love with her. A twinkle came to Yolanda's eye, for she had fallen for him as well.

54

Out of the dark, the old man came forth. He sensed Captain Chris was smitten with the girl, and he was not going to stand for it. "Be gone you foolish man," he yelled. Captain Chris looked at the old man and rose to his feet. They were both looking toward each other in tense silence when Captain Chris quietly muttered, "Father?" The old man stood still for a moment, and with a tear in his eye he nodded yes.

"You see, I had to pretend that I went crazy. They were going to get rid of me," his father explained. "Pirates had overrun my ship. They captured me and threw me overboard in a dingy with a pirate sign on the side. When the people found me, they did not listen. They kept calling me a pirate and were determined to get rid of me. Pretending to go crazy scared them enough to leave me alone."

58

Having talked the night away about the past, they began to discuss a way that the three of them could leave the Isle of Rumors, for Captain Chris's crew were few and rumors of mutiny were abound. "Are you sure the plan will work?" asked Captain Chris's father. "Don't worry as long as you do exactly as we've discussed," said the captain. "Well, can the crew be trusted?" his father asked. There was silence, for no one knew for certain, only time would tell.

60

Two figures approached the dock. It was Captain Chris and what appeared to be a fellow crewman. Two men nearby spotted them and one shouted out, "Who goes there?" "It is I, Captain Chris, and my first mate," said the captain. As they walked by, one of the two men seemed to hide his face from Captain Chris. The captain thought he recognized the man, but he was in a hurry, so he ignored this and pressed on with Yolanda by his side.

62

The man who hid his face from the captain was a former crewman of his. He was said to have fallen overboard during the storm by those who still remained. Moreover, none of the crewmen were actually lost at sea. The missing men hid onboard, then snuck ashore and started rumors about Captain Chris being a deceiving and vicious pirate. These crewmen were determined on having the locals capture their captain so that they may have his ship.

64

During that time on the island, rumors did spread far and wide. They left on other ships, spreading from island to island. Lucky for Captain Chris, he left the craftily named Isle of Rumors before he could be caught. He, his father, Yolanda, and a few honest crewmen set out to sea.

As they sailed across the sea, a flag blew wildly overhead. It was a large, red flag with a half moon in the middle. The ship was heading to where captain Tourik's son lived. Captain Chris stood proudly on the bow, not knowing the many rumors had reached the very island he was about to set foot on.

From the island, the only thing visible was the waving flag. An old man on the docks, recalling the flag, yelled out, "Hey, it's Chris Masss… Mas…" But before the old man could finish the captain's last name, a crowd began to jeer and scream, "Pirate! He's a pirate I tell ye!" A woman, confused in the situation, yelled, "He's the Christmas Pirate?!" Also confused, the crowd began to grow silent in wonder.

The large ship heaved towards the island like it was in a race to save the day. Waves pushed up and over the bow, trying to hold her off. The anchor plunged into the water as the mighty ship came to a halt. People gathered around the dock, all trying to get a glimpse of the Christmas Pirate. Loudly, a voice exclaimed, "I have a gift here for the son of Captain Tourik!" Many children ran to the ship in excitement. A crewman, in sight of this, yelled out to the captain, "Sir, there seems to be more than one."

Quickly, Captain Chris ordered that all trinkets and treasures he had collected over the years were to be thrown into a sack and hauled on deck. The captain jumped up on the rail and shouted to the gathering children below, "Well, come and get your gifts!" As the children ran aboard, a man in the crowd cried, "Well, I'll be… he *is* the Christmas Pirate!"

Captain Chris, now the Christmas Pirate, turned to tip his hat to the man, when he saw a young man standing alone in the cheering crowd who looked eerily like Captain Tourik. The Christmas Pirate climbed down and walked toward him. Silence fell as he asked the young man his name. He looked to the captain and said confidently, "My name is Christopher Tourik, sir."

The Christmas Pirate dropped to a knee, slid out a beautiful golden compass from within his coat pocket, and presented it to the boy. This gift was just for him, as promised long, long ago.

RING